*Look Who's
Playing First Base*

# Look Who's Playing First Base

### by Matt Christopher
*Illustrated by Harvey Kidder*

LITTLE, BROWN AND COMPANY
Boston · Toronto · London

ISBN 0-316-13933-5 (hc)
ISBN 0-316-13989-0 (pb)

Library of Congress Catalog Card No. 74-129907

HC: 10 9 8 7 6
PB: 15 14 13 12 11 10 9

MV NY

*Published simultaneously in Canada
by Little, Brown & Company (Canada) Limited*

Printed in the United States of America

*Look Who's*
*Playing First Base*

# 1

THE BOY was tall, dark-haired and left-handed. He was new in the neighborhood. He lived in the same ten-story brick apartment building that Mike Hagin lived in, but so far Mike hadn't had a chance to talk with him. All Mike knew was what Art Colt had said. Art was a close friend, and if anything new happened within ten miles of Plainview, Art would be the first to hear about it.

"He's from Russia," Art had said. "His father's a teacher."

"Can he speak English?"

"I don't know. I haven't talked with him. But he goes to our school. So does his sister."

"What's his name?"

"Yuri something."

That was all Art could tell him.

Then came the day when Mike was walking home and saw Yuri throwing a hard rubber ball against the side of the apartment building and catching it on the first bounce. Twice the ball struck a curved narrow ledge about three feet above the pavement and rebounded to Yuri without touching the ground. He seemed to be playing a game.

Suddenly the ball struck the ledge again and bounced over Yuri's head, too high for him to catch. It struck the hard pavement behind him and bounced toward the

4

swimming pool about a hundred feet away.

Mike could see that Yuri wouldn't be able to get it before it plunged into the water, so Mike ran after the ball as hard as he could. The ball dropped into the pool just as he reached the pool's concrete deck.

He looked around and saw Yuri running forward, a grin on his round, handsome face.

"It won't sink," said Yuri. "Anyway, thanks for trying."

Mike returned the grin. He was shorter than Yuri, and stockier. "There's a long pole here somewhere with a net on it," he said. "I'll look for it."

"Oh — thanks."

Mike found the pole behind the concrete wall on the opposite side of the pool. It was about ten feet long and big around as a broom handle. The net on the end was used to clear leaves and bugs from the water.

Mike scooped up the ball and held the net up to Yuri, who took out the ball and thanked Mike again.

While Mike put the pole back, he saw that Yuri was waiting for him.

"I'm Mike Hagin," he said. "I live up on the sixth floor."

Yuri put out his hand and Mike took it. "I am Yuri Dotzen. I live on the fourth floor. We just moved here a few days ago." He had a foreign accent but his English was clear. "I go to Plainview School."

Mike smiled. "So do I! Maybe we can go together."

Yuri's eyes warmed. "That would be

nice. I have a sister, too. Anna. She is younger than I."

"Maybe she knows my sister, Ginnie," said Mike. He frowned thoughtfully. "Yuri, are you really from Russia?"

Yuri laughed. "Of course. We moved to the United States a year ago."

Mike looked into the dark brown eyes. "You speak English pretty well."

"That is because I learned it in school. So did my sister. And my parents speak it most of the time at home."

Russia. Man, Russia was halfway round the world. Mike could see the map of Europe in his mind and the huge country of Russia occupying most of its eastern part. The Union of Soviet Socialist Republics. The country that had launched Sputnik, the first satellite to orbit the earth.

"You ever going back?" he asked.

8

"I don't think so. We like it very much here." Yuri laughed and ran toward the apartment building. "Did you ever play this game? One point for catching a first bounce, two for catching it in the air."

"No. But I'll try."

"You must try to hit that ledge," advised Yuri. "If you hit it squarely, the ball will fly back to you in the air. If you miss a catch, it's my turn."

The game was simple, and Mike caught twelve bounces and two flies before he missed.

They started to walk to school together the next day, and their sisters tagged along. The girls were in the same grade but, like Mike and Yuri, had different homerooms.

Then one day Mike heard that the Moodys were moving out of Plainview, which meant that the Checkmates, the team Mike played on in the Bantam Baseball League, were losing their first baseman. Bill Moody was a long string of a kid and left-handed. He could scoop up low throws and pull down high ones as if he were born to do just that. Without Bill the Checkmates had small chance of having a decent team.

*I wonder if Yuri plays baseball?* Mike thought.

"Yuri, did you ever play baseball?" Mike asked him a couple of days before the Moodys left.

Yuri shrugged. "I played last year. I enjoyed it, but I am not the best player. Maybe the worst."

"Did you play first base? Our first baseman, Bill Moody, is moving away, and we'll need a first baseman."

10

"No. I played outfield." Yuri's brows lifted. "Do you think that maybe I can play first base? It looks like a hard position."

"You're tall and left-handed," said Mike. "Lefties make the best first basemen. If you want me to, I'll talk with Mr. Terko, our coach."

"When does the league start?"

"We have two weeks of practice which starts next Monday. Our first game is the following week."

Yuri's eyes lit up. "You think he would let me play first base, Mike?"

"Why not? I can't think of anybody else who'd fit there. Maybe Mr. Terko can — I don't know. But right now I can't."

# 2

IT WAS a perfect day for baseball. Sunny and warm. It was a day when Mike Hagin wished that everything would go smoothly.

He was afraid it wouldn't though. He had that feeling.

He stood at the sixth-story apartment window and looked out at the Little League ball diamond a quarter of a mile away.

The bleachers stretching behind third base and behind home plate to first base were empty now, but later this afternoon most of them would be filled. The green grass and the white foul lines looked like fresh paint.

The swimming pool in the park next to the apartment building was chock-full of yelling, screaming, happy kids. Two life-guards sat in their towers on each side of the pool and watched the swimmers with close attention.

Mike spotted his sister, Ginnie. She was wearing a blue and white striped bathing suit. Even as a ten-year-old, she could swim like a fish.

He lifted his eyes and saw, far off in the distance, the hazy skyline of New York City. It was a forty-five-minute ride by bus from Plainview to New York.

He heard footsteps and suddenly a hand rested on his shoulder. "Well, are you a little excited?"

Mike turned and smiled. His father was a big man with dark hair and warm, brown eyes. He spoke often of his baseball playing days with the Plainview Tigers.

"A little, I guess," admitted Mike.

"What kind of a team have you got this year? Pretty good?"

"Pretty good."

"You don't sound very enthusiastic."

Mike shrugged. He took a deep breath and let it out slowly. "Well, our regular first baseman left."

"Bill Moody?"

Mike nodded. "They moved out West."

"Yes, I know," replied his dad. "But there must be another kid in the neighborhood who can take his place, isn't there?"

Mike shrugged. "Yeah," he said halfheartedly.

He moved away from the window. "You and Mom going to the game?"

Dad grinned. "Wouldn't miss it for the world."

Mike started toward his room. "I'll get dressed."

His mother was ironing in the kitchen. She was a fraction of an inch taller than he and wore her brown hair short.

"Were you able to see Ginnie in that crowd?" she asked.

"Yes. She's the one doing the most yelling," he said.

He changed into his baseball uniform. *Checkmates* was printed in red script across the front of the jersey and number 12 in big print on its back. He pulled on his cap and walked out, carrying his infielder's glove and baseball shoes.

Two floors down he knocked on a door. No one answered and he knocked again. He waited awhile, then went on down. That's funny, he thought. Where was Yuri?

He met Art Colt, Don Waner and Bunker Ford outside. Together they headed for the baseball field. Art was a skinny kid with black-rimmed glasses. He was the Checkmates' starting pitcher. Don was catcher and Bunker played third.

"Where's Yuri?" asked Art.

"I don't know," replied Mike. "Nobody answered the door when I knocked."

He was glad that no one asked anything more about Yuri. He suspected that Yuri Dotzen might be a touchy subject for a while. Those two weeks of practice hadn't been enough to develop him into half the first baseman Bill Moody was.

Coach Bob Terko was already at the field, removing brand-new baseballs from their boxes. He was short, slightly bald, and taught at the Plainview Junior High School.

"You're pitching this opening game, Art," he said, tossing a sparkling white baseball to him. "Here you are. Warm up with Don. Take it easy. I don't want you tired before the game starts."

Don walked with Art to the left of the third-base coaching box and began warming up the right-hander.

Mike played catch with Bunker and Dick Wallace. Dick, short and broad-shouldered, was the team's shortstop.

Mike gave little thought to their oppo-

17

nents, the Maple Leafs. There was no sense wondering how tough they were. The Leafs were probably thinking the same thing. They had shown up and were using the first-base dugout. Some of them already had started batting practice.

Later the Leafs got off the field and the Checkmates took over. At Mike's turn at the plate he belted three pitches to the left side of the batting practice pitcher, then bunted down the third-base line.

He was relaxing in the dugout when Yuri Dotzen appeared, looked at him and waved. "Hi, Mike," he greeted.

Mike's brows shot up. "Yuri! Where were you? I knocked on your door."

"I was with my mother," explained Yuri. A tuft of brown hair stuck out from underneath the brim of his baseball cap.

"We were buying groceries. And my watch stopped. Am I very late?"

"You missed batting practice."

"Well, I had plenty of it the last two weeks."

*Plenty, but not enough,* thought Mike.

"Okay, men!" shouted the coach. "Out on the field! Hop to it!"

Mike saw Yuri look questioningly at the coach.

"First base, Yuri," said Coach Terko. "What're you waiting for?"

Yuri grinned and trotted out to first. Just then Mike heard a comment from someone in the bleachers. "Hey, look who's playing first base. The kid from Russia."

# 3

THE CHECKMATES had their infield practice, then gave the field up to the Maple Leafs. After the Leaf pitcher threw his warm-up pitches, the umpire brushed off the plate and shouted, "Play ball!"

Standing in front of the Checkmates' dugout, Coach Terko announced the first three batters. "Wallace! Hagin! Rush! Get some hits, boys!"

Dick Wallace put on a protective helmet, selected a bat from the fanned-out pile on the ground and walked to the plate. He batted right-handed.

He let the first pitch go by. A strike. The next two were balls. Then he corked the two-one pitch high out to center field.

The Checkmate fans let out a quick yell. It changed instantly to a groan as the ball dropped easily into the center fielder's glove. One out.

Mike was up next. He felt jittery. He always did the first time up. He fouled the first pitch into the third-base bleachers, then waited out the next three throws. They were all balls.

"Go the limit, Mike!" shouted Coach Terko.

The next pitch breezed in and Mike swung. Another foul. In came the three-two pitch. Mike started to swing, then held up.

"Ball!" cried the ump and pointed to first base.

Mike breathed a sigh of relief as he dropped the bat and trotted to first.

Hank Rush, the left fielder, batted next. He wore thick glasses without which he could barely see. With them he could catch any ball he was able to get to.

*Smack!* He socked the first pitch a mile into the air. It came down near the pitcher's mound, where Lefty Mason, the Leafs' pitcher, caught it for the second out.

Center fielder Tom Milligan had no luck, either. He drove a hot grounder to third and was thrown out by four steps.

Mike scooped up his glove from the roof of the dugout and ran out to his position at second base. The Leafs' lead-off man, a right-hand hitter, stepped to the plate.

22

Mike saw Yuri standing almost on top of first base and shouted to him, "Get away from the bag, Yuri! Back up a little!"

Yuri moved several steps to his right and then back. "Come on, Art!" he yelled.

Mike grinned, bent over with his hands on his knees, and took up the chatter.

Art's first pitch missed the plate for ball one. His next missed, too. His third was over. The Maple Leaf then drove the two-one pitch for a single over short.

A bunt advanced him to second base. Art fielded the ball and threw out the hitter. One out.

The next batter flied out, bringing up the cleanup hitter. He batted left-handed and Mike saw Yuri take two steps closer toward the foul line. *That-a-boy, Yuri,* he thought.

*Crack!* A hot grounder down to first!

The ball bounced up, skimmed past Yuri's glove and over his shoulder to the outfield. Mike's heart sank.

"Yuri!" yelled Don Waner. "You playing baseball or tiddlywinks?"

Mike shot a burning look at Don, then saw Yuri's face turn red as a ripe tomato. It had started. Just what he was afraid of. Hot-headed Don was popping off already.

"Forget it, Yuri!" cried Mike. "Get the next one!"

He turned, caught the throw-in from right fielder Dave Alberti, and relayed it home to Don as he saw the runner, who had been on second, sprinting for the plate. The runner stopped short and bee-lined back to third. Don's throw to Bunker was high and the man was safe.

The fifth batter poled a long fly to center. Tom Milligan backed up a few steps, and missed it. Tom pegged the ball in but the runner on third scored. Art struck out the next hitter for the third out.

"I'm sorry I missed the ball," Yuri apologized when he came into the dugout.

"You were nervous," said the coach. "Don't worry about it. There'll be more coming your way. Ford! Dotzen! Alberti!" He read the names from the list he was holding. "Waner! Colt!"

Bunker put on a protective helmet, stepped to the plate and poked the first pitch over second for a clean single.

"Lay it down, Yuri," advised Coach Terko softly.

Yuri nodded. He stepped to the plate, held his bat up as if he were going to drive the ball into the New York skyline, then brought it down into bunting position as the pitch came in. A foul tick. Strike one.

He got into position again, digging his toes into the dirt to brace himself. In came the pitch. Quickly he shifted his position again to bunt.

Another foul tick. Strike two.

"Swing at it, Yuri!" cried Coach Terko.

*Hit that ball, Yuri!* thought Mike as he watched from the dugout. *Drive it a mile!*

The pitch. Yuri cut hard and missed.

"Oh, no!" cried Don, his voice low and harsh. "He can't hit! He can't field! What can he do?" He looked at Mike sourly. "You can really pick 'em, Mike."

"Okay, Don," snapped the coach. "Cool it. We needed a first baseman and Mike thought that Yuri could fit the bill. He's tall and he's not that bad at the plate. I'm going to give him a chance."

Don shook his head. "He'd better improve before too long," he muttered, but

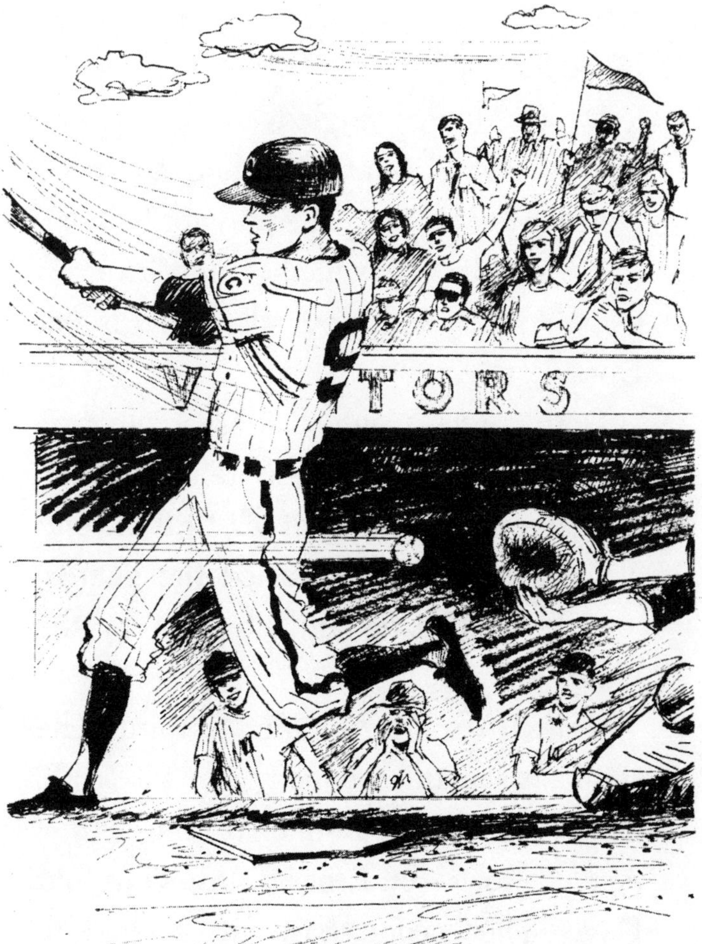
TORS

Mike was sure everybody on the bench heard him.

Dave Alberti singled on a one-one pitch, driving Bunker around to third. Don started for the plate and got halfway to it when Art Colt yelled to him, "Are you going to bat with your shin guards on, Don?"

Don laughed, which was a surprise. You'd think that after his temper flared he'd give up laughing, at least till the end of the game. He unbuckled the guards, tossed them aside and stepped to the plate.

*Crack!* A solid grounder to third! The third baseman scooped up the ball, glanced briefly at Bunker on third, then pegged to second base, throwing out Dave. The second baseman pegged to first, but Don beat it out. Bunker started to run home, then scooted back.

Art flied out to left, ending the top half of the second inning. The Maple Leafs still led, 1 to 0.

Art struck out the Leafs' lead-off man. The second batter popped out to short and the third lined a drive so straight to Bunker that you could have hung clothes on it. Bunker caught it for the third out.

"All right, let's break the ice," said the coach. "Dick, start it off."

Dick Wallace did. He drove a flaming grounder through the pitcher's box for a single. Mike's sacrifice bunt put him on second and in scoring position. Hank, the big gun, popped up the two-two pitch for the second out.

Tom Milligan waited out Lefty Mason's

pitches for a three-two count, then lambasted a belt-high pitch to deep left for two bases, scoring Dick. Bunker singled Tom in for the second run, and up came Yuri Dotzen.

"Keep it rolling, Yuri!" yelled Coach Terko.

"Drive it out of the lot!" cried Mike.

On the mound Lefty Mason took his stretch.

# 4

"STRIKE!"

Yuri stepped out of the box, rubbed his hands on the bat, and stepped in again. The pitch blazed in. Yuri swung. Foul.

"Strike two!"

Lefty hurled one in low and outside for ball one. The next was in there and Yuri cut at it. A low, sharp drive to left. Foul.

Again he hit, and again it went foul. Then he drove one high into short left field. The Maple Leaf fielder got under it and took it for the third out.

Mike started to rise from the bench and

31

a hand gripped his arm. It was Don Waner's. "You know what, Mike?" he said. "If that friend of yours doesn't come through soon I'm going to throw in my gear. The Crickets need a catcher. It isn't too late for me to join them."

Mike's face colored. "You can't do that, Don. Yuri will come through. Give him a chance."

"Chance? He's lousy, Mike. He won't get any better and you know it." He hopped out of the dugout before Mike could say another word.

The first Maple Leaf batter laced Art Colt's chest-high pitch for a double. The next dropped a bunt toward third, fooling the Checkmates completely. The play drew a big laugh from the Maple Leaf fans. The runner on second made it safely to third and the bunter safely to first.

"Don," said Coach Terko, "tell Bunker to come in a little. Watch for another bunt."

A slow grounder to second! Mike ran in, grabbed the hop, glanced at the runner on third, then pegged to first. The throw was low, but if Yuri stretched he'd be able to catch it.

Yuri didn't stretch. He tried to field the hop and missed it. The ball squirted past him toward the foul line and a run scored.

"Yuri!" shouted Art angrily. "You would've had it if you stretched!"

Mike shook his head and socked the pocket of his glove with his bare fist. He looked at Don. The catcher was standing with his back to the field, his arms crossed. Some of the Maple Leaf fans were chuckling.

"Must've been hard up to get him, huh, Don?" said one of them.

Whatever Don's answer was Mike couldn't hear, but it sure brought a big laugh from the fans.

The runners had advanced to second and third. Art Colt took his time on the mound and Mike could see that he was shaken. He grooved a pitch. It was fouled over the backstop screen. His next two pitches were balls.

The batter hit the two-one pitch to deep center. Tom Milligan pulled it in and pegged it to Dick Wallace, who relayed it home. But the runner on third had tagged up and beat the throw to home by several steps.

The runner on second advanced to third.

"Come on, Art!" yelled Mike. "Sock it to 'im!"

A high hopping grounder to Yuri. *Don't miss it, Yuri! Don't miss it!*

Yuri caught it. Mike saw the runner on third make a beeline for home. "Home, Yuri!" he yelled.

Yuri had taken a step toward the first-base sack, but suddenly he stopped and pegged the ball home. It was high — too high for Don to reach.

"What do you think I am? A giant?" cried Don.

The ball sailed into the backstop screen and the runner scored.

*I knew something lousy was going to happen,* thought Mike. *I just knew it.*

A pop-up to short and a fly to Tom Milligan ended the half inning. Checkmates 2, Maple Leafs 4.

The coach motioned to Yuri. "You're

pretty shaken up, Yuri. Sit out the rest of the game. I'll have to work you more on grounders. You've got the arm but not much control." The coach turned to a tall, slender boy who was just leaving the dugout to coach at first. "Bob, play first the next inning. Better warm up."

"Okay, Coach." Bob Layton wasn't bad on grounders, but he was weak at bat. Even Yuri, thought Mike, could hit better than he.

Mike looked up and his eyes locked with Yuri's. Yuri shook his head sadly. And then he looked at Don. "It's about time," muttered Don.

"Don!" snapped the coach. They looked at each other, the coach's eyes glaring.

"Sorry," said Don. He leaned over, unbuckled his shin guards, then picked up a couple of bats and began swinging them back and forth over his shoulders.

I wonder if he would quit and join the Crickets, thought Mike. He'd be mean enough to, and leave us without a catcher. Not another guy on the team had ever caught before. And it was no easy position. Mike remembered that he had tried it once and even with all that protective gear he was afraid when a batter swung. It was the same with the other players. Don was the only catcher they had. If he left, the Checkmates might as well fold up.

"Cy," said the coach, "bat for Dave. Gary, coach at first." Gary Roberts was the Checkmates' alternate pitcher.

The top of the fourth. Cy Williams, a red-headed kid with hair growing over his ears, took a called strike and two balls, then belted a pitch to center. The Maple Leaf fielder caught it for the first out.

Don Waner, up next, swung hard at the first pitch. *Crack!* Like a shot the ball zipped out to deep left. Don dropped his bat, rounded first, then second, and was held up at third for a neat triple.

Art Colt hit a sharp single through the pitcher's box and Don scored. Dick Wallace smashed a line drive to the shortstop. The Leaf snapped the ball to first in an effort to pick off Art, but Art got back in time.

Mike fouled off two pitches to the left of the third-base sack, then drilled a line drive over the second baseman's head. The ball bounced past the outfielders, scoring Art, and Mike held up at second. The hit made him feel good. Almost to the point of smiling were not the thought of Yuri at the front of his mind.

He perished there as Hank Rush struck out.

Checkmates 4, Maple Leafs 4.

Art mowed down the first hitter. The second laced a line drive to Bunker Ford. Bunker raised his glove and ducked. He seemed surprised to find the ball in the glove's pocket. The next Leaf popped to first to end the bottom of the fourth inning.

Tom Milligan and Bunker failed to hit in the fifth. Bob Layton singled, followed by another single off Cy Williams's bat. Cy had pinch-hit for Dave Alberti. The ball was just out of the shortstop's reach and Bob was forced to hold up at second.

"Get two!" yelled the Leaf infielders as

Don Waner came to bat for the third time.

"Strike one!" A blazing pitch over the inside corner.

"Strike two!" A ball that drilled the heart of the plate.

"Ball!"

"Ball two!" Was Lefty Mason losing his control?

And then — *crack!* A smashing drive to third. Don slammed the bat down and bolted for first.

The third baseman missed the ball. It bounced up against his chest and rolled in front of him. He sprinted after it, picked it up and pulled his arm back to throw to first.

"No, Bert! No!" yelled the shortstop.

The Leaf held the ball. Bob, who hadn't moved far off the third-base sack, now returned to the base and stood on it till the third baseman tossed the ball to Lefty.

Three men on, two outs, and Art Colt was up.

It was a chance to go ahead of the Leafs.

# 5

LEFTY MASON'S first pitch was low, almost hitting the back of the plate. the Leafs' catcher trapped it in his mitt.

"Ball!" cried the ump.

The second pitch was outside. "Ball two!"

The third pitch was high for ball three. The Leaf catcher called time and trotted out to the mound to have a word with Lefty. A few seconds later he trotted back. Lefty stepped to the mound again. He pitched.

"Strike!"

Art stepped out of the batter's box, yanked at his belt and protective helmet, then stepped in again.

"Strike two!"

The Leaf fans roared. Then all was quiet as Lefty went into the motion of delivering his next pitch. It was in there and Art swung. A long drive to deep center field! The runners were advancing. The center fielder went back . . . back. The ball seemed to be sailing over his head.

And then the outfielder jumped, his glove high over his head, and pulled the ball down. Three outs.

No one had received a louder ovation than did the Leaf player as he raced in from the outfield. Lefty Mason and other Leaf players thumped him happily on the back.

Mike was grim as he grabbed his glove

from the dugout roof and hustled out to second. He caught a wiggling grounder from Bob Layton and pegged the ball back hard and high. It was too high, sailing far over Bob's head.

He was thinking of Yuri, wondering if he had made a mistake in asking Yuri to try out for first base. It would be bad enough that the guys would never let him forget it if Yuri didn't come through once in a while. It would be worse if Don held to his threat to quit.

Yuri had to come through, or the Checkmates might as well throw in the towel.

Mike was sick thinking about it. He had never realized that playing baseball could turn out to be so miserable at times. For the first time he wished that he had never met Yuri Dotzen. Don Waner was temperamental, but he was just about the best catcher in the league. The Checkmates couldn't afford to lose him. But what could Mike do about it now? He couldn't ask Yuri to quit. *Maybe if I was Don I could,* Mike thought. *But I'm me. I can't ask a guy to play and then ask him to quit. That's crazy.*

The lead-off hitter for the Leafs punched a Texas league single over third. The next batter tried to bunt and fouled the pitch.

"Come in closer, Bunk!" yelled Don to the third baseman.

Bunker moved up to the base path. At first base Bob Layton stood in front of the bag, holding the runner on.

Art delivered. A smashing grounder to short. Dick Wallace scooped it up and pegged to second. A bad throw! Mike took two steps off the bag to catch the ball, then rushed back and touched it just in time to force out the runner advancing from first. It was too late to make the play at first base.

The next batter, a left-handed hitter, laced the first pitch through the hole between Bob and Mike and slid into second base for a double. The throw-in from right fielder Dave Alberti was a fraction of a second late as Mike caught it and pressed the gloved ball against the runner.

The Leaf player got to his feet, brushed the dust off his pants and smiled. Mike knew him. He was Tom Kearny.

"The kid who played first base — Yuri Dotzen," said Tom, squinting against the sunlight. "Heard he's Russian."

"He is," said Mike, and frowned. That spark of amusement in Tom's eyes meant that he had more to say about Yuri.

47

"You and he are pretty buddy buddy, aren't you?" Tom went on. "Ginnie and Yuri's sister, too."

Mike's eyes flamed. The ball slipped out of his glove and dropped. "So what?" he snapped angrily, stooping to pick up the ball and peg it to Art in the same motion. "They're good kids. What's wrong . . ."

Just as Mike threw the ball, Tom bent over and the ball struck him squarely on the side of the helmet. He staggered off the base, lifting a hand to his head.

"Time!" shouted the base umpire, running forward.

Mike ran up to Tom, scared stiff. "Tom! I didn't mean it! You stooped over just as I —"

"You and your communist friends!" snarled Tom. "You did it on purpose!"

"You're crazy! You bent over just as I threw the ball!"

"I was going to tighten my shoelaces," said Tom.

The Leaf coach came sprinting forward. "Tom, are you hurt?"

"No. I'm all right. It just made my ear ring."

"Are you sure?"

"I'm sure."

The coach glanced at Mike, his eyes questioning, but he said nothing. He slapped Tom gently on the rear and walked off the field.

Mike looked across the diamond at Yuri standing at the side of the dugout and saw a look of despair on Yuri's face. He must have heard Tom's remark. Tom had said it plenty loud.

Boy, it was one thing after another. It was bad enough to contend with Don, a member of his own team. He had to contend with an opponent, too. *Darn it, Yuri! Why did you ever come to Plainview? Why didn't you stay back there in your old Russia?*

The game resumed. The Leaf batter lined a hit over first, scoring a run. Tom held up at third. Art fanned the next. A pop-up to short ended the bottom half of the fifth inning. Checkmates 4, Maple Leafs 5.

Mike trotted off the field, tossed his glove onto the roof of the dugout and found a vacant spot to sit far from where Yuri was standing. He didn't want Yuri to start asking questions.

The Checkmates' dugout turned into a beehive as the game went into the last inning. Dick Wallace led off with a long fly to left field. It was caught. Then Mike singled. So did Hank Rush, sending Mike around to third. The Checkmates and their fans began yelling like mad. A good, long drive could put them ahead.

Tom Milligan cracked a slow grounder to third. The Leaf third baseman fielded it, saw that he couldn't get Hank at second so pegged to first, getting Tom out by two steps. Mike took several steps off third and rushed back.

Two outs and Bunker was up. Lefty looked at him nervously. He removed his cap and mopped his brow. He pitched, couldn't get one over and Bunker walked.

Three men on and Bob Layton was the hitter. Lefty breezed in the pitch. "Ball!"

He blazed the next two across the plate, then threw one so wide the catcher had to jump out after it. The two-two pitch blazed in. Dick swung. Strike three!

The game was over. The Maple Leafs won, 5 to 4.

"We almost won," Yuri said to Mike. "I suppose we would have if I had not made those stupid errors."

"Forget it," said Mike. "It was just our first game. Come on. Let's go home."

They started away from the dugout.

"Mike, that boy you had hit on the head — I heard him say something about 'your communist friend,'" said Yuri. His voice caught. "I am not a communist, Mike. I never was. None of my family were."

Mike looked at him, saw the honesty etched plainly on Yuri's face. "I don't think he meant it, Yuri."

"But he said it. Mike, we came to the United States to get away from communism. It is almost impossible to move out of Russia. The government hardly lets anyone travel out of the country, but we were given a permit to travel. Once we were here my parents decided to stay."

Mike had wondered why the Dotzens had come to the United States, but he had figured it wasn't his business to ask. Now Yuri was telling him why.

"It was hard to leave our relatives and friends," he went on. "But my parents decided that it was best for us. For Anna and me."

Someone came up beside them. Mike recognized the Leaf coach. With him was Tom Kearney. Then Coach Terko approached, followed by Bunker, Don and Art.

"Yuri, I'm Bud Adams," said the Leaf coach, a square-jawed, deep-chested man.

"I heard what Tom said out there. You may have, too."

Yuri nodded, blushing. "I was just talking with Mike about it," he said softly.

Tom stepped up to him. "I'm sorry, Yuri. I didn't mean what I said."

"That's okay," replied Yuri. "Forget it."

"I'd like to say something here," said Coach Terko, looking at the group that had formed around them. "Baseball is a sport. It's a game in which we all try to become better ballplayers than we are. And it's a great game because it stresses two very important things: skill and sportsmanship. Work on those two. Develop them and you'll find out that nothing else belongs. Politics has nothing to do with it. Nothing else matters but the game. Put that in your heads and keep it there. Okay. Let's go home."

# 6

MIKE and Art Colt went to the pool the next afternoon. The place was crowded. The day was hot and sunny and it looked as if every kid who lived in the apartment house was there.

Don Waner and Bunker Ford were there, too. They sat at the edge of the pool in their trunks and talked about yesterday's game.

There was a sudden clapping of hands accompanied by cheers, and the boys looked to see what it was all about. A girl's head popped out of the water and she started to swim with long overhand strokes toward a diving board. She looked real young. As she climbed out of the pool Mike recognized her.

"That's Anna," he said. "Yuri's sister."

"Dive again, Anna!" one of the kids shouted.

They watched her climb up to the platform of the high diving board. She walked to the end of it, turned halfway around and moved her feet to the very edge. Then she dove, pulling her knees up against her body as she spun through the air. At the last instant she straightened out and pierced the water with barely a splash.

"Hey, man!" cried Bunker. "She's okay!"

"She's won five or six medals for diving," said Mike.

"How good is Yuri at it?"

A shadow crossed Mike's face and he looked up. "Here he is," he said. "Ask him."

Yuri smiled. "Ask me what? If I can dive like my sister?"

He was wearing blue trunks. They were still dry.

"Can you?" asked Bunker.

Yuri shrugged. "Some other time. Some people may think we are showing off."

He turned and made a shallow dive into the pool. He swam underwater for several yards, came up, then swam with long, graceful strokes to the side of the pool where a small throng had gathered.

Mike stood and saw Anna Dotzen in the center of the throng. He wasn't surprised to see Ginnie next to her. They were pretty good friends. The boys walked over to them. Yuri had already reached the group and was sitting on the edge of the pool, looking at his sister.

". . . They are called the Young Pioneers," she was saying. "Yuri was a member. I would be too if I was there."

"How old must you be to be a member?" someone asked.

"From nine to fourteen," replied Anna. "At fourteen they join the Komsomol. But I don't know anything about them."

"Do you have a summer vacation like us?"

"Oh, yes. From June till September. Just like it is here."

"But we have no Christmas or Easter holidays," explained Yuri, and everyone's eyes turned to him. "Near New Year's Eve we get a tree which we call the winter tree, and Father Frost brings us gifts."

"Father Frost?"

"Yes." Yuri and Anna laughed. "Here he is called Santa Claus," said Yuri.

"What is the Komsomol, Yuri?" asked Art.

"An organization for boys and girls from fourteen to seventeen," answered Yuri. "They are taught about the Revolution and communism. It — it's too complicated to talk about."

He stood and took his sister's hand. "Come on, Anna. I promised Mama one swim and I would bring you home."

# 7

O N JUNE 29 the Checkmates had last raps in their game against the Jetstars. Gary Roberts was on the mound for the Checkmates and Ike Pierce, a right-hander, for the Jetstars.

The infield seemed quiet as a cemetery as the first batter stepped to the plate. Mike could understand why Yuri wasn't making noise; Yuri was still shy. But what was the matter with Dick Wallace and Bunker Ford? Even Don Waner, who controlled his throws much better than his temper, was silent.

"Come alive, men!" he shouted. "Let's hear ya!"

The shout brought them to life. They all started yelling at once. A smile flickered on Mike's face. A pitcher felt better when his men talked to him. You had to give him vocal support, not just physical.

Gary stretched and delivered. The ball shaved the edge of the plate for strike one. The next pitch grazed across the inside corner for strike two.

Gary kept the next two pitches wide, probably hoping the batter would bite at them. The Jetstar didn't bite. Two more pitches and he walked.

The next batter blasted a hard liner right to Gary. He caught the ball and whipped it to first, nabbing the runner before he could tag up. Just like that — two outs.

A pop fly to short ended the top of the first inning. Dick Wallace started off with a walk. Mike laid down a sacrifice bunt, advancing Dick to second. Then Hank Rush singled to right, scoring Dick. The ball was pegged in to second base, holding Hank on first.

Tom Milligan cut at the first two pitches, then fouled off two. The Jetstars' Ike Pierce couldn't get the next three over and Tom was faced with a three-two count. Ike grooved the next pitch and Tom belted it for a single over short. Hank raced around to third.

Two on. One out.

Bunker swung hard at a low pitch and drove the ball sky-high. The third baseman caught it for out two.

Then Yuri came up and Mike heard Don say, "Here we go. Another out."

The hair on Mike's neck bristled. *Darn you, Don. You just don't want to give him a chance.*

Yuri took a hard swing at the pitch and fouled it off to the right field bleachers. *Come on, Yuri,* Mike pleaded silently. *Make Don eat his words.*

Strike two. Another foul.

Ball!

Another hard swing. This time Yuri didn't even tick the ball. Strike three.

"There you go," said Don. "What did I tell you?"

Mike glared at him. "That was just his first time up, dope. He's coming up again."

"Oh, sure," Don snorted. "And he'll whiff again, too."

The Checkmates held the Jetstars scoreless in the top of the second, and picked up their second run during their turn at bat. With one out Don had singled and gone to second on a sacrifice fly to deep right field, then had scored on Dick's double.

The Jetstars' lead-off man in the third popped a high fly just inside the first-base line. Yuri got under it and stood waiting for it while the crowd watched silently. Even Mike held his breath. Then the ball hit Yuri's glove — and bounced out.

Mike groaned, looked at Gary then at Don. It was Don who worried him more than anyone else. He almost expected the catcher to throw off his mask, chest protector and shin guards then and there.

Yuri picked up the ball, waited for Gary to turn around, then tossed it to him. "I'm sorry, Gary," he said.

Gary struck out the next batter, then

walked the following two men, filling the bases. Mike called time and trotted to the mound. "You okay, Gare?" he asked.

"Oh, sure," grumbled Gary, kicking the soft dirt. "I feel great."

"Shake it off. We can't win if you stay sore, Gary."

"I'll be okay."

A hard belt to left center field! One run scored! Two runs scored!

Tom Milligan pegged the ball in to third. Bunker caught it. He took a few paces toward the mound and tossed it to Gary. "Not your fault, Gary," he said.

A strikeout and a grounder ended the inning.

The Checkmates came back hot as fire. Hank doubled on the second pitch, then Tom Milligan did what every Checkmate fan hoped he would do. He knocked one that just cleared the left field fence for a home run. Bunker walked and the fans yelled for Yuri to keep it going.

"Ha!" Mike heard a snort. He didn't have to look to know where it had come from.

*Please, Yuri,* he pleaded. *Lambaste that ball. For me.*

The pitch. Yuri swung and missed. "Strike one," muttered Don.

The second pitch came in. "Strike two," Don muttered again. But he said it before Yuri swung. *Crack!* Yuri's bat met the ball solidly, driving it out like a little white pill and up into the sky where, it seemed, it was going to be swallowed by a cloud. Then it curved and started to drop fast, so far out that Mike was sure it would never be found again. It cleared the fence for a

home run — the longest home run Mike had ever seen hit on this baseball field.

The Checkmate fans roared, and Mike jumped up and shouted, "That-a-boy, Yuri! I knew you could do it! I knew it!"

Don Waner had nothing to say.

Dave Alberti singled, and time was called while the Jetstar coach and a couple of his infielders walked up to their pitcher to offer him some voice support. For a minute Mike thought that the coach was going to send Ike Pierce to the showers, but he didn't. Ike stayed in and the fans cheered.

Don was the next batter. *Now let's see what you can do, Mr. Big Shot,* thought Mike. Ike didn't pitch Don anything good. He didn't pitch him anything bad, either. Don went the full count, three and two.

He stepped away from the plate, hitched up his pants and stepped into the box again. Ike's pitch came in, slightly high. Don belted it.

A long drive to left! Don dropped his bat and tore for first. When he was almost there the first-base coach raised his hands and shook his head. The fielder had caught the ball. Without looking toward the outfield Don trotted back to the dug-out.

Both Gary and Dick made outs, too.

But the Checkmate fans were applauding them, and Coach Bob Terko looked pleased. "Nice going, boys. Let's hang on to that lead."

The score was 6 to 2, Checkmates' favor.

The first Jetstar batter singled. He then took a lead off first which, thought Mike, was just too much. The guy didn't intend to steal, did he? Not with the Jetstars trailing by four runs?

The pitch came in. "Ball!"

The runner didn't steal. But Mike saw that he was taking his sweet old time returning to the base. He hoped that Don wouldn't be caught napping and let the man steal.

"Strike!"

The instant Don caught the ball he rose from his crouched position and whipped it hard to first. Yuri stretched wide, caught it and reached out to tag the runner. Instead, the runner bolted for second. Yuri chased after him, then tossed the ball to Mike. Mike chased the runner back toward first, then tossed to Yuri. Again Yuri went after him, and again he threw the ball to Mike.

This time he threw it wild. The ball struck the runner on his head, dropped to the ground, and the Jetstar ran safely to second.

Mike's temper exploded. "Yuri! Why'd you do that for? We had 'im in the bag!"

Yuri just looked at him, his eyes still as glass.

# 8

THE JETSTAR batter was husky, broad-shouldered, and kept twirling his bat around and around slowly, his eyes watching Gary like a cat's.

Mike looked across at Yuri, feeling the anger slowly slipping away from him. He and Yuri could have made an easy out if Yuri had had better control of the ball.

*I don't know,* he thought. *Just when I think he's getting better he pulls a dumb play.*

Gary stretched and delivered. The ball

72

grazed the inside corner of the plate. The batter started to swing, then changed his mind. Strike one.

Gary's second pitch was knee-high and almost dead center over the plate. The batter swung and the ball shot out to right center for a clean hit. The runner on second scored and the batter raced to second base on the throw-in to home.

That was it for the Jetstars that half inning.

Mike was wiping his brow with a handkerchief in the dugout when Yuri plunked down beside him.

"Gary said I could have caught up with that boy and tagged him out," he said.

Mike shrugged. "Maybe you could have and maybe you couldn't. But if you had thrown the ball straight . . . Aw, forget it. Don't sweat it."

"Oh, sure. It could be that easy for you. But it isn't for me."

Mike looked at him. Yuri was holding his cap on his lap. Beads of sweat covered his forehead and his black hair was matted down. But it was his sad, pale eyes that showed how he really felt.

"This is only our second game," said Mike softly. "Stick in there and don't worry about what somebody else says. It's what Coach Terko says that's important. Okay?"

Yuri smiled. "Okay."

"Mike, you're first batter," piped up Coach Terko. "Don, coach at third."

The boys hopped out of the dugout. Mike slapped on a helmet, picked up a bat and hurried to the plate. He socked the second pitch for a line drive through short for a single. Cy Williams, pinch-hitting for Hank Rush, poked the first pitch in a looping fly behind short. It looked like a hit, but the Jetstar shortstop raced back and caught the ball over his shoulder.

The Jetstar fans gave him a big hand.

Mike ran back to first. Tom Milligan then drilled the ball through the hole between first and second and Mike raced around to third.

Bunker Ford, up next, popped the first pitch to the catcher. He dropped it! Bunker fouled off another pitch for strike two, then waited out the pitches for a three-two count. Ike Pierce grooved one belt-high and Bunker lined it out to short center field. The fielder sprinted after it, caught it and pegged it in, holding both runners on their bases.

Mike waited for Yuri to bat, but Coach Terko was talking to him. What was he going to do — have someone pinch-hit for Yuri? Then Yuri walked to the plate, swinging his bat back and forth.

"Cork another one over the fence, Yuri!" shouted Mike.

"Oh, come on, Mike," grunted Don, standing in the coaching box. "Twice in one game? Aren't you asking for too much? That first homer was just lucky."

"Lucky? You still don't think he's a good sticker, do you?"

"He hits like he fields," said Don. "Now and then he catches a grounder or a fly. Now and then he pops a homer."

"*Pops* a homer?" Mike's forehead creased. He pointed to right field. "You call that long blast popping a homer?"

Don shrugged. "Like I said, he was lucky."

"Oh, man," said Mike. "You sure cut the cake, Don. You sure do."

Yuri swung at the first pitch and missed. He took two balls. Then *crack!* Another real long clout to deep right! Everybody on the bench jumped out and watched it. Everybody in the stands and the bleachers just sat silently and stared as if something had happened to their voices. The blast was almost like the first one, heading like a rocket for the clouds and then dropping fast and landing far on the other side of the right field fence.

And then came the explosion. The yell from the crowd, from the Checkmates. Mike clapped his hands so hard they hurt. He turned to Don and saw him looking at

his shoes. Mike smiled. For a while, at least, Don won't be threatening to quit. He didn't have a good reason to, now.

Dave Alberti struck out. Checkmates 9, Jetstars 3.

The Jetstar lead-off man blasted Gary's first pitch for a double, and the hit seemed to start them off for something good. The next Jetstar clouted a pitch to right center, driving in a run.

Then Gary couldn't seem to find the plate and walked two men in a row. Don called time, trotted out to the mound and talked to Gary for a few seconds. Gary was sweating as if someone had poured a bottle of water over him.

The talk did little good, if any. The batter drove a long fly to left field. It was caught, but a man ran in for the Jetstars' second run of the inning. Then Dick Wallace snapped up a hard hit grounder, fired it to Mike at second, and Mike rifled it to first. A double play. Three outs.

Don led off in the bottom of the fifth. He spat on his hands, rubbed the bat and then faced the pitcher as if he were going to blast the ball even farther than Yuri did. The pitch came in. Don swung, and if his bat had connected squarely with the ball his wish might have been granted. But the bat struck the top of the ball, resulting in a hopping grounder through short for a single.

Next came Gary. He waited out the pitches, then popped a fly to third. Dick Wallace fouled two pitches before striking out.

Two outs and Don was still on first. Mike got up and poled a long foul past the left field bleachers, then straightened one out for a double, scoring Don.

The Checkmate fans were still cheering Mike's drive when Cy Williams corked the first pitch for a long triple, a blow to left center, scoring Mike.

It was a blow to Ike Pierce, too. His coach sent him to the showers and put in another pitcher, a tall right-hander with glasses. He faced Tom Milligan and that was it. Tom hit to center field for the third out.

Checkmates 11, Jetstars 5.

Top of the sixth. Gary seemed to have lost sight of the plate again and walked the lead-off man. The Jetstar runner was like a bumblebee as he hopped back and forth on the base path.

Gary took his stretch, then suddenly

shifted toward first and drilled the ball to Yuri. Yuri tagged the runner as he slid back to first in a cloud of dust. Safe.

The next instant Mike saw Yuri hopping on his left foot.

"Time!" yelled the base umpire.

Coach Terko sprang out of the dugout. Yuri waved him back. "I'm okay," he said. But a look of pain was on his face.

"You sure?" asked the coach.

"Yes. I'm sure."

Yuri hobbled around a bit, then tossed the ball to Gary and returned to cover first base. Time-in was called and the game resumed.

The Jetstar runner began hopping back and forth again. Gary kept his eyes on him, then shifted his attention to the plate and fired. He worked up to a two-one count on the batter, then was hit for a

single to right field. Mike ran out to shallow right, got the relay from Dave Alberti and pegged to Bunker. The Jetstar on first had raced around to third and slid under Bunker's reaching glove. Safe.

A fly to deep center was caught, but the runner scored. Mike was almost relieved that the Checkmates didn't have to contend with that guy anymore.

A pop fly and a strikeout finished it for the Jetstars, who wound up trailing 11 to 6.

"Don says he's quitting," said Bunker as he, Mike and Yuri headed for home.

Mike paled. "He's just talking."

"I don't think so. I think he means it. I know he's a sorehead, but do you realize that if he quits we don't have a guy to take his place? Nobody else wants that position. I don't, not even if you paid me."

# 9

SINCE their next game was sched-
uled for Monday, July 6, the Checkmates practiced every afternoon during
the rest of the week except the weekend.
And Don was present every day. But he
was quiet. If he intended to stick to his
threat of quitting he wasn't saying any
more about it.

Yuri worked hard to improve his playing at first base. Mike could see that he
was trying his best.

The coach had the infielders practice
trapping a runner caught in a hot box. He

had Bunker play the runner trapped between first and second and gave Yuri the ball. Yuri ran Bunker down to second, while Gary Roberts backed him up. Then Yuri, not able to catch up with Bunker, threw the ball to Mike, who ran Bunker back toward first. This time Mike threw to Gary, while Yuri ran to back up Mike.

Pretty soon Bunker was pooped out and Yuri tagged him out.

"Get the idea?" smiled Coach Terko. "Three men are all it takes to trap a runner."

Yuri's face broadened with a grin. "What a wonderful idea!" he exclaimed.

The Checkmates played the Crickets on Monday and led by a fat margin, 5 to 0, till the fourth inning, when a grounder ripped through Yuri's legs. Three men were on and two of them scored. The

Crickets picked up their third and fourth runs in the sixth.

Mike suffered the nightmare of what the guys — especially Don — would have said if they hadn't had those five runs to back them up. As it was, Art Colt and Bunker Ford ignored Yuri completely after the game.

Don didn't. "Better start looking for another catcher," he said to Mike. "I've got another team lined up."

"Not the Crickets?"

"No, not the Crickets. It'll be another week — maybe less — then I'm leaving you bunch of clowns."

"Where are we going to look? And who else can catch? Nobody. You can't just drop us like that."

Don looked belligerent. "Oh, no? Just wait and see if I can't."

On Wednesday Mike Hagin himself almost gave the game to the Rascals. The score was 3 to 1, Checkmates' favor. It was the fifth inning and there were no outs. The Rascals had a man on first. The batter blasted a grounder to second and Mike flubbed it. He scooted after the ball, whipped it to Dick covering second, and the ball sailed far over Dick's head. Bunker chased after the ball beyond the foul line, pegged to Art Colt covering third, and his throw was wild too. Before all the throwing was done a man had scored and a runner was on third base.

A single then tied up the score. Two pop flies and a strikeout stopped the Rascals' wild merry-go-round.

The Checkmates picked up two runs in the sixth, and that was it. Checkmates' game, 5 to 3.

The Longhorns fell too. The game was better than the five-to-one score looked, though. The Longhorns got their loner in the first inning, while the Checkmates pushed one across each inning. Once it was on a squeeze play. Another was a long fly Yuri blasted to center field. He was really hitting the ball. And once on an error by the shortstop. Two runs were batted in by doubles.

It was the first game in which Yuri had not made an error.

"I guess I am improving," he said to Mike, smiling proudly. Then he added, "Mike, we have already played five games and lost only one. Maybe we will be champs."

"Don't count your chickens too soon," said Mike.

Yuri frowned. "Chickens?" Then his

face lit up. "Oh! I know what you mean!"

Lefty Mason was on the mound again for the Maple Leafs when they played the Checkmates. Don was there. Maybe he's pulling our leg, thought Mike. He's just making those threats and has no intention to quit at all. A big blowhard, that's all he is. Yuri came to bat in the second inning. There were two outs and Bunker was on first base after hitting a single.

Lefty's first pitch cut the outside corner of the plate for a strike. His second was inside — so far inside that Yuri had to jump back.

Lefty's next pitch was almost in the same place. Yuri jumped back again and stared hard at the Leaf pitcher.

Mike, coaching at third, looked on curiously. Was Lefty having trouble with his control or did he really mean to dust Yuri off?

"Strike two!" The ball grooved the heart of the plate. Mike saw Yuri step back slightly.

*That darn Lefty Mason,* he thought. *What's he trying to do?*

The pitch. Yuri stepped back again and took a weak swing at the ball. He missed it by a foot.

"Strike three!"

The Checkmates ran out, the Leafs ran in. Mike glared at Lefty but said nothing. *Wait'll I get up,* he thought.

The Leafs blasted Art Colt's pitches for two runs. The Checkmates came to bat, Dave Alberti leading off and Don Waner on deck.

Lefty's control was fine as he pitched to

Dave. None of his throws were so close that Dave had to jump out of the way. Dave singled to left.

Don corked a Texas leaguer over short. Art Colt flied out and Dick walked, loading the bases.

Mike came up. He eyed Lefty squarely as he held his bat off his shoulder, moving it just slightly back and forth. Lefty stretched and delivered. The pitch came in. It was high. Ball one.

The next pitch blazed in close. So close that Mike dropped to the ground.

"Ball two!" shouted the ump.

The next pitch grazed the inside corner for a strike.

Mike stepped out of the box, brushed off his pants and looked sharply at Lefty Mason. *Okay, Lefty. You'll either walk me or groove the next pitch. And if you groove it I'll murder it.*

He stepped back into the box and waited for Lefty's next pitch.

# 10

LEFTY MASON stretched high, came down with the ball and held it a second as he glanced at Dave on third base. Dave was leading off a couple of feet.

Lefty pitched.

The ball blazed in like a comet. Mike could see it was going to be a perfect strike. He leaned into it and swung.

*Crack!* The sound was like a shot as bat met ball. And like a shot the ball zoomed out to deep left. It seemed to rise higher the farther it went. Mike dropped his bat and sped to first. Something about the feel of the bat when it had struck the ball told him the hit was real solid.

Cy Williams, coaching at first, was smiling broadly and windmilling Mike on. Then Mike saw the ball drop far behind the left field fence. He slowed his pace and trotted around the bases, the roar of the crowd ringing in his ears.

He had done it. He had murdered Lefty's pitch just as he had promised he would. It was the best feeling he'd had in months.

Hank went down swinging, but Tom Milligan doubled to put the Checkmates into scoring position again. Bunker singled him in. That was all the Checkmates were able to do that inning. It was plenty. Checkmates 5, Maple Leafs 2.

Two innings later, in the top of the fourth, tragedy almost struck. Mike missed a pop fly, a spinner. No sooner had it hit the pocket of his glove than it spun out. The next batter drove Art's first pitch for a triple, scoring a run. The third batter blasted a hot grounder to deep short and the runner on third made a beeline for home.

Dick Wallace fired the ball to Don. It was a good throw. But the runner was almost in and Don moved his mitt to tag him before he had the ball. The ball glanced off the side of his mitt and skittered to the backstop screen. The runner slid safely across the plate.

The Checkmates picked up a run in the bottom of the fourth and another in the fifth, putting them ahead of the Leafs by three runs.

In the top of the sixth a Leaf blasted a hard grounder through short for a neat single. The next Leaf hit a high-bouncing grounder to first.

"Get two, Yuri!" shouted Mike.

Yuri waited for the ball, then reached for the hop. The ball struck the heel of his glove and bounded off his chest to the ground. He picked it up quickly and raced the hitter to first base. The hitter beat him by two steps.

Mike's lips tightened. Both he and Yuri were really having a great day in the field, all right.

Well, with men on first and second there was still a chance for a double play.

A solid hit to right center! The ball rolled to the fence. Center fielder Tom Milligan got it and pegged it in. Two runs scored and the hitter ran to third standing up.

Checkmates 7, Maple Leafs 6.

Art struck out the next batter. The next blasted a line drive over third and another run scored — 7 to 7. Art caught a pop fly for the second out. Then a grounder tore down the first-base line and Yuri bolted after it. The ball struck the tip of his glove and bounded out to right field for three bases, putting the Leafs ahead, 8 to 7.

Mike looked at Dick, at Bunker, then at Art. It was plain as day that they were completely disgusted. Yuri should've caught that grounder. *The only thing that keeps Yuri in the game is his bat*, thought Mike. *And, boy, Yuri, you'd better make sure it does something for you the next time you're up.*

A fly to short ended the half inning.

Yuri was quiet as he walked in from first

base. He dipped himself up a drink from the water pail, then paused beside Mike as Mike looked for his favorite bat.

"I should have caught that one," he said regretfully. "It looked easy."

"Get a hit and make up for it," said Mike quietly. He went up to bat and let a strike and a ball whizz by him. Then he knocked a dribbling grounder to the pitcher for an easy out.

Hank Rush flied out to center and Tom Milligan popped out to the catcher, for a fast half inning to end the game.

"We can't win 'em all," said Mike as he helped Coach Terko load up the equipment bag.

"No. But one error should've been an easy out," grumbled Don Waner. "We should've won the game."

"Okay, let's drop it," said the coach.

"There's another game coming up. Let's think about that one."

Yuri and Mike exchanged few words between them as they headed home. The wide sidewalk flanked a park sparsely dotted with trees and bushes.

"Do you think Don is serious about quitting?" asked Yuri worriedly. "I heard he said that. And it is because of me."

"I don't think so," said Mike. "He's just a bag of wind. Don't listen to everything he says."

*I hope I'm right,* thought Mike. *I hope that's all Don is — a bag of wind.*

# 11

THE CHECKMATES had an easy time winning over the Jetstars on the 23rd. Mike knocked his second home run of the season, with two on, and Yuri blasted one out of the lot too. He had missed a high pop fly but nobody said anything about it.

On July 29 the Checkmates had first raps against the Rascals. They drew a goose egg. The Rascals came to bat and their lead-off man cocked a looping fly just over Dick Wallace's head for a Texas league single.

102

The second Rascal batter drove a pitch directly back to Gary. The hard-driven ball glanced off Gary's glove toward first base. Yuri fielded it and tagged out the runner two steps from the bag.

The third Rascal popped a fly just outside of the first-base foul line and Mike waited breathless as Yuri got under it. The ball dropped from the sky — and Yuri caught it. A load left Mike's chest, and Checkmate fans gave Yuri a rollicking cheer.

The fourth batter cracked a double and drove in a run. The fifth walked. Another double drove in two more runs. Three to nothing.

A solid blast to deep center! The Rascals were really pounding the ball. Tom Milligan went back . . . back . . . and bagged it.

Three outs.

Tom received the loudest cheer ever as he trotted in from the outfield, the ball clutched in his hand.

"Nice catch, Tom," said Mike. Then he sat down beside Yuri. "Nice catch, Yuri."

"Thanks," said Yuri. "All the time that ball was falling, though, I was worried."

Mike laughed. "So was I!"

The second inning went by scoreless.

Dick Wallace drew a walk to lead off the top of the third inning. Mike grounded out to short and Hank fanned. Then Tom doubled, scoring Dick, and Bunker struck out. Checkmates 1, Rascals 3.

The Rascals' lead-off man drove a hot grounder directly at Yuri. Yuri reached down and the ball struck the heel of his glove. He recovered it too late to put out the hitter.

"Yuri!" shouted Don. "Why don't you sit in the dugout? You may do better there!"

"Don!" yelled the coach from the bench. "Keep your mouth shut!"

A pop fly and a quick double play ended the Rascals' chance of scoring.

Yuri was first man up in the top of the fourth. He looked nervous. Mike was sure that the last error and Don's sarcastic remark were responsible. *Just ignore him, Yuri. You should know him well by now. He's just a bag of wind.*

Fergie — Hayes Ferguson — hurled in the first pitch and Yuri backed away. "Strike!" boomed the ump.

He's still worried about getting hit by a pitched ball, thought Mike. Lefty Mason was to blame for that.

"Strike two!"

Mike felt his heart pound as if he were

at the plate himself. He wished he were. He wouldn't feel as tight or anxious.

"He's some pal," said a voice at his elbow. A familiar voice. "You sure can pick 'em, man."

Mike sucked in his breath and let it out slowly. Then he looked at Don and smiled. "Don," he said, "did anyone ever tell you how nice a guy you are?"

Don grinned. "Very funny," he said.

Fergie stretched and delivered. The crowd was silent as the ball shot like a bullet toward the plate. Yuri drew back his bat, brought it around as he leaned into the pitch. Then *boom!* A long, high, sky-reaching blast! The crowd started to shout almost the same instant that Yuri's bat connected with the ball. The shout seemed to grow louder as the ball climbed higher. And then the ball, like a white pill, dropped far beyond the fence, while the crowd kept cheering and cheering. Yuri loped around the bases, a broad smile on his face as he crossed the plate and came in to the dugout.

One by one the guys shook his hand. Even Bunker, Art and Don did, except that they didn't seem as enthusiastic about it.

Mike's grip of Yuri's hand was probably the hardest. "Beautiful hit, Yuri!" he said happily. "You can really swing a mean bat!"

Cy Williams, batting for Dave Alberti, singled. Then Cy stole second, and scored on Don's single over second base.

The Rascals failed to do a thing during their raps, and neither team scored in the fifth. In the top of the sixth Don doubled to left center, for his third hit of the game, and Gary drove him in. He was real quiet. Any other guy would be tickled pink to have gotten three hits. If Don was, he didn't show it. Mike knew what the trouble was. Don was jealous. Even three hits in a game couldn't match the spirit the crowd displayed when Yuri had blasted that long home run.

Bob Layton, pinch-hitting for Dick Wallace, grounded out. Mike pounded out a single, scoring Gary, the second and last run that half inning.

"Hold 'em, Checkmates!" yelled the fans.

The Checkmates did, and won, 5 to 3.

That evening came the news. It was a phone call from Coach Terko.

"Don Waner handed in his uniform, Mike," he said. "We're out of a catcher."

Mike could hardly believe his ears. "I

— I was beginning to think he was just talking," he said. "I didn't think he'd do it."

"I didn't, either. I think he talked himself into it, Mike. He said it so often that he figured if he didn't quit now the guys would say he just talks and never backs up his word."

"That could be, Coach."

"Don's a good kid and everybody likes him. But he has a strong sense of pride. I tried to make him change his mind, and even bawled him out for blaming Yuri for losing our games. You guys play baseball because you enjoy the game. I coach it because I love it. But you learn to get along with one another and that winning or losing is just a part of it."

"Maybe Don hasn't learned that yet, Coach," said Mike.

"It's just his stubborn pride, Mike. Well, now comes the tough part. I'd like to ask a favor, Mike."

"Sure, Coach."

"I'd like you to take Don's place. Until he comes back — *if* he comes back."

Mike gulped. "Sure, Coach. I — I'll do the best I can."

# 12

MIKE HAGIN crouched behind the plate during batting practice to get acquainted with his new position. The mask felt like a basket over his head. And peering through it — well, he had a good idea now how a caged canary must feel.

The chest protector and shin guards seemed to weigh a hundred pounds. And the huge mitt — How did Don ever do it? How could any catcher ever do it?

But that was only half of it. The other half was his being scared whenever a batter swung at the ball. Mike was all right as long as the batter didn't swing. When the batter swung he just couldn't catch and hold on to the ball. He didn't know what made him scared. Maybe he was thinking more about the batter's swinging than he did about catching the ball. He wasn't sure. Anyway, he dropped almost every pitched ball whenever the batter swung.

But, if *he* didn't catch, who would? No one. Some of the guys were even more scared to catch than he was.

The big day arrived. The day he caught his first game. It was against the Crickets and Mike thought he had never been so nervous in his life.

He crouched behind the plate, peering through the cage of his mask and feeling the heavy weight of the chest protector and shin guards. "Come on, Art!" he shouted, pounding his fist into the pocket of his huge mitt. "Right in here, boy!"

Art's first pitch was head-high. Mike couldn't get the mitt up fast enough and the ball sailed over his head to the backstop screen. He chased after it, wondering how in the world catchers could run so fast with all that weight on. He picked up the ball, pegged it to Art and trotted back to his position.

Somehow the Checkmates got the batter out, and then the next two. The Crickets picked up two runs in the second and one in the third. *We're heading for a real bombing,* thought Mike unhappily. His glove hand was hurting, too. The small flat sponge Coach Terko had given him to cushion the blows didn't help much.

In the bottom of the fourth his hopes went up as Yuri came to the plate with the bases loaded. One of Yuri's long clouts could put the Checkmates ahead like the snap of a finger. With each pitch the crowd seemed to hold its breath, as if it too were thinking the same thing.

"Strike one!"

"Strike two!"

"Ball!"

And then . . . *whiff!* Yuri struck out! The Cricket fans went almost crazy.

In the fifth Mike himself started a rally and the Checkmates picked up two runs. In the top of the sixth the Crickets picked up two more, putting them in the lead, 5 to 2. Then, during the Checkmates' last raps, Yuri stepped to the plate. Again the bases were loaded. And again the crowd hushed as the first pitch breezed in.

Ball! For a moment a hum rose, sounding like a thousand bees. Then it hushed again as the next pitch came in. *Crack!*

"There it goes!" yelled Mike.

And it did. A grand-slammer! The Checkmates won, 6 to 5.

This time it was the Checkmate fans who shouted like crazy.

Things were different on Thursday. Mike missed a couple of pop flies that were hit directly over his head. The other Checkmates just didn't seem to have the spirit to play ball and the Longhorns smeared them, 8 to 3.

"Wish Don would come back," said Bunker. "We need him." He grinned at Mike. "I don't mean to be rude, Mike. And it's not because we lost. We just — well, we just miss him. That's all."

Mike smiled faintly. "I know. I do, too."

The Longhorns lost to the Crickets on Wednesday, but beat the Checkmates again on Thursday and the Rascals on Tuesday, giving them seven wins and five losses. Up till the nineteenth, the Checkmates' record was seven wins and four losses. If they lost to the Rascals they would be tied with the Longhorns and would have to meet in a playoff game.

"Has anybody seen Don?" asked Yuri as he sat with Mike beside the swimming pool the evening before the Checkmates' last game.

"I haven't," said Mike.

"Is he playing baseball with some other team?"

Mike shrugged. "I haven't heard," he said.

"I should have quit, not he," said Yuri softly. "It has been my fault — his quitting."

"Forget it," said Mike. "The season's almost over."

"Sure. And everybody will remember Yuri Dotzen, the Russian boy. They will say his poor playing made a good catcher quit the team and made the team lose the championship. That is what everybody will remember."

Mike slid off the edge of the pool to the ground. "You talk too much," he said. "Come on. Let's go home."


Most of the Checkmates were at the field when Mike and Yuri got there. The sun was hiding behind an overcast sky.

Mike's palm was still swollen and sore from catching. The sponge he used hadn't helped very much. Each of Gary's throws felt like a hot iron falling against his hand.

*I'll never be able to catch three innings, let alone six,* he thought wretchedly. *My hand already looks like a raw hamburger.*

Just then a kid came around the corner of the dugout. A familiar kid. He wasn't wearing a uniform, but he was carrying a glove and a pair of baseball shoes.

It was Don Waner.

# 13

COACH TERKO looked hard at Don. "Do you think you deserve to play in our last game of the season after what you did?" he asked, his voice as hard as his look.

Don cleared his throat. "No. No, I don't."

"But you still would like to play?"

"Yes."

Mike looked at Bunker, at Art, at the other guys, and then at Yuri. They were waiting anxiously — waiting to hear Coach Terko's decision.

"Did you try to get on another team?"

Don's eyes lowered. "No."

"Why not? I thought you wanted to."

"I changed my mind. I didn't want to get on another team."

There was silence for a while. A good long while. Then Don said, "I couldn't play with anybody else, Coach. These guys — they're my friends. All of them. Yuri, too. I — I really didn't mean all that stuff I said about him." He looked at Yuri. His eyes were red. "I didn't, Yuri."

Yuri smiled. "That's okay, Don."

"No, it isn't. I got to thinking about it. And I — I realized how stupid I was. Boy!" He shook his head. "I don't know. Here I've been with the best bunch of guys in the whole world and I had to pull a stupid stunt like that. But I kept saying I'd quit, unless . . . well — that stuff I said about Yuri. I didn't want to go back on my word. Even when I did it I was sorry."

"You were thinking of your pride," said the coach.

"Yeah. My pride."

"Then you really are sorry for what you did?"

Don opened his mouth. Nothing came out. He just nodded.

A grin splashed over the coach's face and he slapped Don on the back. "Okay, son. Come on. I'll get you a uniform."

Don's eyes were dim as he looked at the coach, then at the other guys, every one of whom was smiling broadly.

And then he was running after the coach — running to get back into his Checkmate uniform.

The Checkmates had last raps in their

final game of the season. If Fergie, the Rascals' fast right-hander, pitched his usual good game, he could put his team in the winning column. But the Rascals' record of six wins and five losses showed that they seesawed back and forth. How they made out today depended a lot on Fergie.

"C'mon, Gary!" shouted Don, banging the pocket of his mitt. "Give it to me, boy!"

Mike smiled. It was sure good to see Don Waner back with the team.

Gary Roberts breezed in the pitch and the Rascal lead-off man popped it to short for an easy out. The next Rascal grounded out to Mike and the third lined a long fly to Tom Milligan. Three outs. The teams exchanged sides.

Dick Wallace stepped to the plate. Fergie blazed in the first pitch for a strike.

The next pitch was in there too, and Dick blasted it. The ball sailed out to left and was caught for out number one.

Mike, up next, waited for a good pitch and Fergie gave it to him. Mike swung. The hit was a solid grounder to short. The Rascal shortstop fielded the hop and threw Mike out by a mile.

Hank Rush didn't even touch the ball. Fergie mowed him down with three pitches.

Oh-oh, thought Mike. Fergie looks in top form today.

"Blaze it by him, Gary!" he shouted from second base as the Rascal lead-off man stepped to the plate.

Gary Roberts grooved the pitch. *Crack!* The ball pierced the air like a shot, out to deep left. It cleared the fence for a home run and the Rascal fans went wild.

"That blow ought to prick the Checkmates' fat balloon!" yelled a Rascal fan.

It didn't. The next three hitters went down — one, two, three.

Tom Milligan led off the bottom of the second with a free pass to first. Bunker flied out to left, Yuri swished, and Dave grounded out to short.

The Rascals came to bat with fire in their eyes. But the Checkmates chilled them, as again the Rascals went down — one, two, three.

"Let's not blow this game," said Mike. "What's one run? Let's get three or four!"

In spite of the Checkmates' trailing he felt the best he had in a long time.

"Okay, Don," said the coach. "You're up. Start it off."

Don removed his catching gear, put on

a helmet and walked to the plate. He took a called strike, then cut hard at the second pitch. The blow was solid, but directly at the left fielder. One out.

Gary grounded out to short. Then Dick walked and Mike came to bat. He blasted a low pitch directly at the second baseman, cussed under his breath and raced to first.

The second baseman flubbed the ball! It bounced over his shoulder and behind him. Mike was safe at first.

Hank was blessed with luck too. The shortstop missed his sizzling grounder. The bases were loaded and Tom Milligan was up.

"Cork it into the next county, Tom!" shouted a Checkmate fan.

His first swing might have done it if his bat had connected with the ball. Instead, it missed completely. The next swing connected solidly.

The ball never climbed higher than twenty-five feet or so, and was caught easily by the Rascal center fielder. Three outs.

The fourth and fifth innings produced no runs either. The single run scored in the second inning by the Rascals loomed bigger than ever.

The Rascal lead-off man grounded out to short in the top of the sixth. The next hitter popped a high fly outside of the first-base line and Mike beelined for it.

"I'll take it!" cried Yuri. "I'll take it!"

The ball dropped into Yuri's glove and stuck there.

"Thataway to go, Yuri!" shouted Mike. His yell was drowned out by the cheers from the crowd.

Gary mowed down the third batter. Three outs.

"All right, men," said Coach Terko. "It's our last chance. Tom, get on."

Tom walked. Bunker then laid into a one-one pitch for a single, and Tom raced around to third.

Yuri was up.

"Blast it, Yuri!" cried Don. "Send it into orbit!"

Mike looked at him and smiled. *I couldn't play with anybody else, Coach. These guys — they're my friends. All of them. Yuri, too.* He was sure Don had meant every word.

Yuri stood at the plate, a calm, unworried look on his face. Fergie grooved the first pitch and Yuri swung. Strike.

He watched the second pitch zip by. Strike two.

*Come on, Yuri!* Mike pleaded. He could see that Yuri had gotten over the fear of being hit by the ball.

Yuri stepped out of the box, put the bat between his legs, rubbed his hands together and stepped in again.

*Crack!* A long, solid blow to deep, deep center! It seemed longer than any ball he had hit before! Another home run!

It was over. The Checkmates won, 3 to 1.

"Man, oh, man, you can really swat that ball!" smiled Don, pumping Yuri's hand.

Yuri smiled through the sweat glistening on his face. "Thanks, Don," he said. "And thanks for coming back, too."

"That goes for me, too," said Mike. "Double!"

# How many of these Matt Christopher sports classics have you read?

## Baseball

❑ Baseball Pals
❑ Catcher with a
   Glass Arm
❑ The Diamond Champs
❑ The Fox Steals Home
❑ Hard Drive to Short
❑ The Kid Who Only
   Hit Homers
❑ Look Who's Playing
   First Base
❑ Miracle at the Plate
❑ No Arm in Left Field
❑ Shortstop from Tokyo
❑ Too Hot to Handle
❑ The Year Mom Won
   the Pennant

## Basketball

❑ Johnny Long Legs
❑ Long Shot for Paul

## Dirt Bike Racing

❑ Dirt Bike Racer
❑ Dirt Bike Runaway

## Football

❑ Catch That Pass!
❑ The Counterfeit Tackle
❑ Football Fugitive
❑ Tight End
❑ Touchdown for Tommy
❑ Tough to Tackle

## Ice Hockey

❑ Face-Off
❑ Ice Magic

## Soccer

❑ Soccer Halfback

## Track

❑ Run, Billy, Run

All available in paperback from Little, Brown and Company

---

# Join the Matt Christopher Fan Club!

To become an official member of the Matt Christopher Fan Club,
send a self-addressed, stamped envelope (#10, business-letter size) to:

Matt Christopher Fan Club
34 Beacon Street
Boston, MA 02108